W9-BKJ-827

To the Lovitt family
and their newest Little Pip, Keely Grace.
She's a good egg!
—K. W.

For Isaac and Daniel

—J. C.

MARGARET K. McELDERRY BOOKS • An imprint of Simon & Schuster Children's Publishing Division • 1230 Avenue of the Americas, New York, New York 10020 • Text copyright © 2010 by Karma Wilson • Illustrations copyright © 2010 by Jane Chapman • All rights reserved, including the right of reproduction in whole or in part in any form. • MARGARET K. McELDERRY BOOKS is a trademark of Simon & Schuster, Inc. • For information about special discounts for bulk purchases, please contact Simon & Schuster Special Sales at 1-866-506-1949 or business@ simonandschuster.com. • The Simon & Schuster Speakers Bureau can bring authors to your live event. For more information or to book an event, contact the Simon & Schuster Speakers Bureau at 1-866-248-3049 or visit our website at www.simonspeakers.com. • Book edited by Emma D. Dryden • Book designed by Lauren Rille • The text for this book is set in Tarzana Narrow. • The illustrations for this book are rendered in acrylic. • Manufactured in China • 1010 SCP • 10 9 8 7 6 5 4 3 2 • Library of Congress Cataloging-in-Publication Data • Wilson, Karma. • What's in the egg, Little Pip? / Karma Wilson ; illustrated by Jane Chapman.—1st ed. • p. cm. • Summary: Little Pip the penguin comes to terms with the presence of an egg, which will soon hatch into a little brother or sister. • ISBN 978-1-4169-4204-7 (hardcover) • [1. Eggs—Fiction. 2. Penguins—Fiction. 3. Animals—Infancy—Fiction. 4. Family—Fiction.] I. Chapman, Jane, 1970– ill. II. Title. III. Title: What is in the egg, Little Pip? • PZ7.W69656Wf 2010 • [E]—dc22 • 2009020331

What's in the Egg, Little Pip?

Karma Wilson illustrated by **Jane Chapman**

Margaret K. McElderry Books
New York London Toronto Sydney

Little Pip stared at the Egg. The large, white oval rested on Mama's feet just under her soft, warm belly. Pip used to sleep there, but there was no room for her now, not since the Egg. Mama and Papa asked, "What do you think, Little Pip?"

Pip shrugged. She wasn't sure.

Mama and Papa had talked about the Egg for a long time.
Yesterday morning they had woken Pip and said,
"The Egg is finally here, Little Pip!"
As they showed her the Egg
they sang this song:

"The Egg, the Egg, the lovely Egg,
a wonderful, glorious sight.
A sister or brother for sweet Little Pip
will soon make our family just right."

Pip frowned. The Egg didn't look like much.

"Our family *is* just right," Pip said. "That old Egg can't make it better."

Mama nuzzled Pip and said, "Just wait. You may be surprised. And now, Papa, it's time for you to take over."

Mama carefully nudged the Egg
and tucked it on Papa's feet.
Then Papa nestled down onto the Egg.

"Where are you going, Mama?"
Pip asked.

"I need to go fish to bring food for you," Mama
said, "but somebody must always be with the
Egg to keep it warm. So Papa will watch the
Egg while I fish, and I will watch the Egg
when Papa fishes."

"Can I go with you?" Pip pleaded.

Mama smiled and shook her head. "You stay and help Papa keep the Egg warm and safe. We must be ready for any storms. We don't want the Egg to get cold. We'll need you."

Pip sighed. "I'm too little to help. I'm still your baby."

Mama shook her head. "You have grown up so much, Little Pip. You're big enough to help Papa. You're big enough to help me. You're even big enough to help the Egg! Remember that. But don't worry; you will always be our baby."

Pip wasn't so sure. As she watched her mama waddle away, a tear slipped down her cheek. Now it was just her and Papa . . . oh, and the Egg.

Later that day Pip chirped,
"Papa, let's slide on the ice."

Papa shook his head.
"I can't leave the Egg, Little Pip."

Pip frowned. "Not even for a minute?"

"Not even for a second."

"But isn't it boring?"

"A little," said Papa.

"Then why do you do it?" Pip asked.

Papa smiled. "That's what families do, Little Pip.
I did the same for you when you
were just an egg."

Pip couldn't imagine that she was ever just an egg.
Why had Mama and Papa even wanted the Egg?
I should be enough! thought Pip.
She wandered off to think, and as
she slumped along she sang,

"The Egg, the Egg, it's all the Egg.
Nobody cares about me.
I liked it best before the Egg,
back when our family was three."

Little Pip felt so all alone that she decided to look for her best friend, Merry. "You want to go slide?" she asked.

"I guess," said Merry. She didn't seem her usual cheerful self.

"Does your family have an egg too?" asked Pip.

Merry nodded and stamped her foot. "I don't see the fuss about the Egg. It just sits there and does nothing."

"I know," said Pip. "But it's all Mama and Papa ever talk about or think about anymore. I want to forget about the Eggs. Let's slide!"

And so they did.

WHOOP!

WHEEE!

WHISH!

They didn't think about the Eggs again.

But suddenly the sun disappeared
behind a thick, black cloud.

"A storm!" squealed Pip.
"We must run! **Hurry!"**

"We're too little," said Merry. "We can't!"

Pip ruffled her feathers and puffed out her chest.
"My mama said I'm big enough to help the Egg.
So are you. We have to go help. Now RUN!"

They raced the cloud all the way home.

Just as they reached camp, frozen sleet started
to fall in cold, stinging drops. Pip snuggled tight
against her papa, helping to shield the Egg.

There they huddled, and there they waited.

And waited.

And waited.

Finally Mama returned. Pip's tummy growled.
She was glad to eat the fish Mama had brought back for them.
But then Papa had to go fishing.

Storms came and went, and the Egg always had to be kept warm. Pip, Mama, and Papa huddled around the Egg for many weeks. Sometimes Mama left to fish, sometimes Papa, but Pip always stayed with the Egg.

Then one bright, sunny day, while Mama was away fishing . . .

CHIP,

CHIP,

CRACK.

"The Egg is broken, Papa!" Pip cried, and buried her head into Papa's chest. All that work, for nothing.

Craaaaaack.

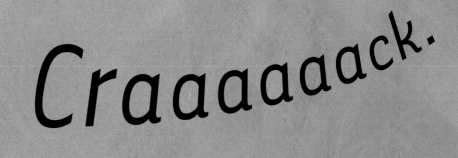

Pip gasped. The Egg was gone.
In its place sat a beautiful penguin chick.

"It's a chick! A chick, Papa!"

"Little Pip, meet your brother."

At the beach lots of penguins were squawking
and talking. Pip saw a flock of penguins
just back from fishing. Mama! She was home.

Mama sighed with happiness. "He looks just like you
when you were a baby, Pip!"

Pip smiled. "I was that small?"

"Oh yes," said Mama. "Just that small."

Pip looked at her new brother and she sang,

"*Welcome, chick, you lovely chick.*
What a wonderful, glorious sight.
Little brother, I name you Sam.
You make our family just right."

Little Pip looked around and saw all the penguin families
snuggling new chicks in their pebbly nests. Pip waved
to Merry and Merry waved back, a huge smile on her face.

Pip smiled too.
Everything felt
just right.

JUN 0 7 2012